Smart George

For Michael,
who counts

Text and pictures copyright © 2020 by Jules Feiffer

Library of Congress control number: 2019942171

HarperCollins Publishers, New York, NY 10007

Printed and bound by Phoenix Color

Designed by Steve Scott

First edition, 2020

20 21 22 23 24 25 PC 6 5 4 3 2 1

George's mother said, "One plus one equals what, George?"

George said, "First, you have to feed me."

So she fed him.

Then George's mother said, "Two plus two equals what, George?"

George said, "First, you have to walk me."

So she walked him.

Then George's mother said, "Three plus three equals what, George?"

George said, "It's time for my nap."

While he napped, George dreamed about numbers.

Two
plus three
equals what, George?
Mother!
Come and tell these trees how much you need me!

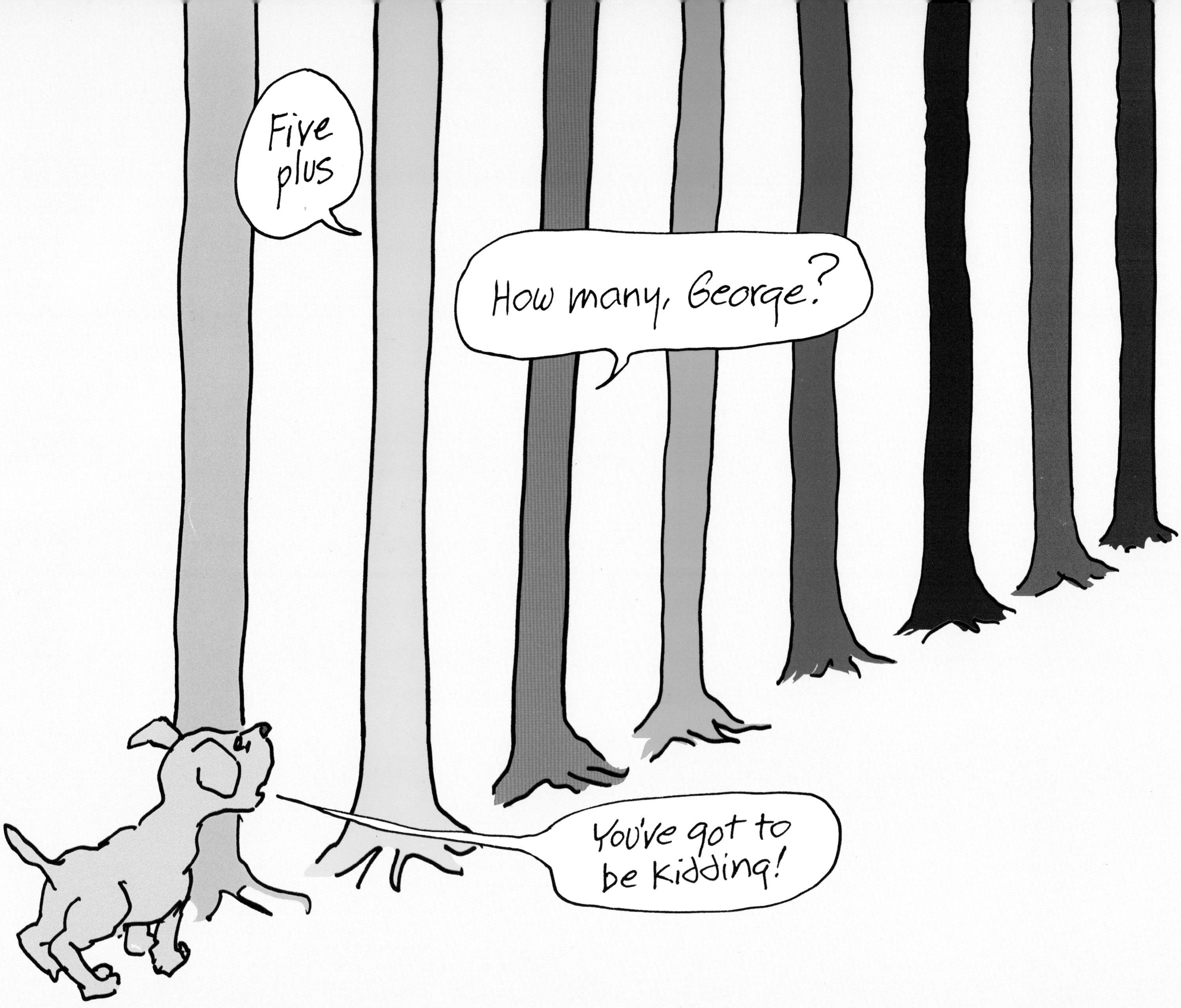
Five plus
How many, George?
You've got to be kidding!